D0985769

This book belongs to:

FOUR LITTLE BUNNIES

Photographs by
HARRY WHITTIER FREES

*Dedicated to all
the little bunnies who posed for
the pictures in this book*

NOTE: These unusual photographs of real bunnies were made possible only by patient unfailing kindness on the part of the photographer at all times.

Once upon a time there were four little bunnies. Their names were Fluff, Puff, Muff, and Algernon. This is the way they looked when they were all dressed up.

They lived with Mother Bunn and Daddy Bunn. Mother Bunn taught them to play quietly. She taught them to eat *all* of their dinner. And she taught them *never* to sniff at nice spinach and carrots. Daddy Bunn taught them to look before they hopped.

One day at breakfast Algernon licked the cocoa off his whiskers and said, "Tomorrow is Easter. I'm going out to find Mother Bunn a present!"

"So am I!" cried Puff and Fluff and Muff, licking the cocoa off *their* whiskers.

(Mother Bunn was upstairs and could not hear them.)

"That's a good idea!" said Daddy Bunn, who was frying himself just one more pancake. "But don't forget to do your work before you go."

So Fluff said, "Yes, Daddy," and took her broom and pail of water and scrubbed the floor.

And Puff said, "Yes, Daddy," and took his lawn mower and cut the grass.

And Muff said, "Yes, Daddy," and hitched up Henrietta the hen to the little red cart and brought back twelve eggs from the hen house.

Algernon said, "O. K., Daddy." (He meant well though he *did* use slang.) Then he put on his old checked trousers and he got out the soap and washboard and a big tub of water. And he rubbed and scrubbed and rubbed and scrubbed and did *all* the family washing.

When they were through their work the four little bunnies kissed their mother and daddy. Then they went hippity-hop down the hill from their hollow-tree home.

Mother Bunn waved good-by to them from the window.

And Daddy Bunn waved good-by to them from the front door.

Then Mother Bunn and Daddy Bunn put their headphones over their ears and listened to the Market Reports on the radio. (Though Mother Bunn liked the Cooking Hints better.)

The first thing Fluff and Puff did was to hurry down hill, hippity-hippity-hippity-hop. And the first thing Muff and Algernon did was to ride down hill on a scooter. The kitten next door went, too, but hopped off by her favorite tree. (She climbed up that.)

At the foot of the hill, Puff and Fluff and Muff and Algernon met their friend White Rabbit, standing in his doorway.

"Bless my whiskers!" cried White Rabbit. "You are just the bunnies I am searching for. Will you look after my babies this afternoon?"

The four little bunnies stood still.

"It's a good deed!" whispered Fluff and Puff and Muff. "And we can find Mother an Easter present later."

"O. K.," said Algernon, and he said it very loud indeed.

"Thank you," said White Rabbit. And he went over to the hammock to take a nap.

"Thank you," said Mrs. White Rabbit, too, as she put on her best hat.

And then she went next door to the wedding of Miss Snowy Ears and of Mr. Cottontail.

So Fluff took care of Millie and Tillie Rabbit. She let them swing in their swing—high-and-low and high-and-low.

And Muff and Algernon took care of Teenie and Weenie Rabbit. They took them out for a ride in their gocart.

And then fed them some nice spinach soup.

White Rabbit woke up. He thanked the four little bunnies again for helping with the children.

"You're welcome," said the bunnies. And they started down the path.

Pretty soon they came to Big Bunny who was tied to a post.

"Please rescue me!" said Big Bunny. "Some naughty boy tied me up, so I can't get away."

"I will!" said Fluff and Puff and Muff. And they gnawed the rope that tied him.

"O. K.!" said Algernon. And *he* gnawed the rope.

"Thank you," said Big Bunny when they had gnawed the rope loose. "I am the Easter Rabbit. Come to my house and you may help make Easter eggs."

"Goody! Goody! Goody!" said Puff and Fluff and Muff.

"O. K.!" said Algernon.

Two rabbits hopped by, carrying eggs in a basket. All the bunnies followed them.

At the Easter Rabbit's house they all put on work clothes. Then Fluff poured colors on the hard-boiled eggs—blue and green and red and yellow and pink.

"It's fun!" cried Fluff.

49

Then Puff dipped the candy eggs in chocolate.

"It's lots of fun!" cried Puff.

Then Muff helped another rabbit squirt chocolate icing on the white eggs. "It's lots and lots of fun!" cried Muff.

Then Algernon squeezed white icing on chocolate eggs and made pretty pictures on them, too.

"O. K.," said Algernon.

Then all the bunnies helped pack up the Easter eggs into wagons to take to children everywhere. They all worked hard.

The Easter Rabbit gave the four little bunnies all the eggs they made. Then they piled these into airplanes.

"Let's - -" began Puff.

"Take them home - -" said Fluff.

"To Mother!" said Muff.

"O. K.," said Algernon.

Algernon made more eggs than the others. He made a candy rabbit, too.

My, he was glad to take them all home!

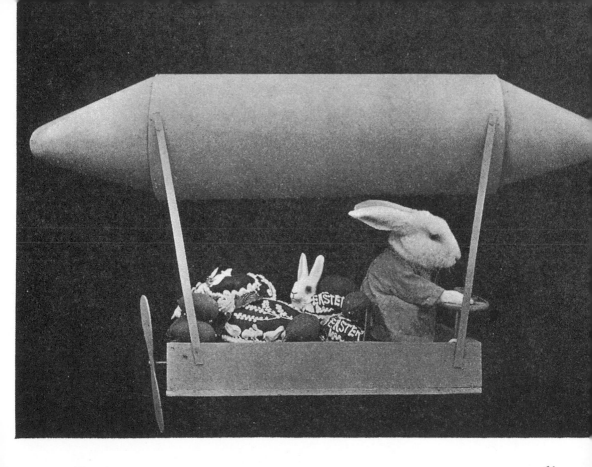

When the bunnies got home there was Daddy Bunn giving Mother Bunn an Easter bouquet. So they gave their present.

Mother Bunn kissed them all.

"What dear, thoughtful little bunnies!" she cried. "I hope you will always be as good as you have been today!"

"We'll try!" said Puff, Fluff, and Muff.

"O. K.!" said Algernon. (And that meant he would try, too.)

**Did You Enjoy
This Story ?
Good !
Now Go To Sleep**